For my dearest Rikka

First published individually as *Where's My Teddy?* (1992) and *It's the Bear!* (1994)

This edition published 1999 by Walker Books Ltd
87 Vauxhall Walk, London SE11 5HJ
for The Book People Ltd, Guardian House
Borough Road, Godalming, Surrey GU7 2AE

2 4 6 8 10 9 7 5 3 1

This book has been typeset in Garamond ITC.

Printed in Hong Kong

British Library Cataloguing in Publication Data
A catalogue record for this book is
available from the British Library.

ISBN 0-7445-6744-0

WHERE'S MY TEDDY?

Jez Alborough

TED SMART

Eddy's off to find his teddy.
Eddy's teddy's name is Freddy.

He lost him in the wood somewhere.
It's dark and horrible in there.

"Help!" said Eddy. "I'm scared already!
I want my bed! I want my teddy!"

He tip-toed
on and on
until …

something
made him stop
quite still.

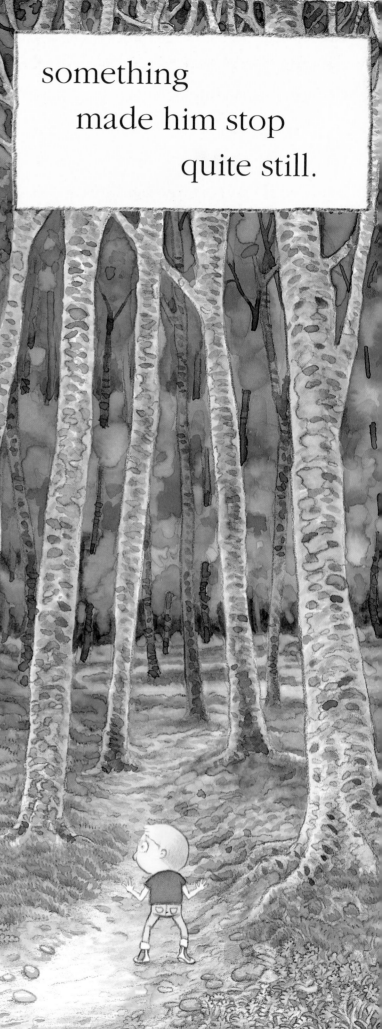

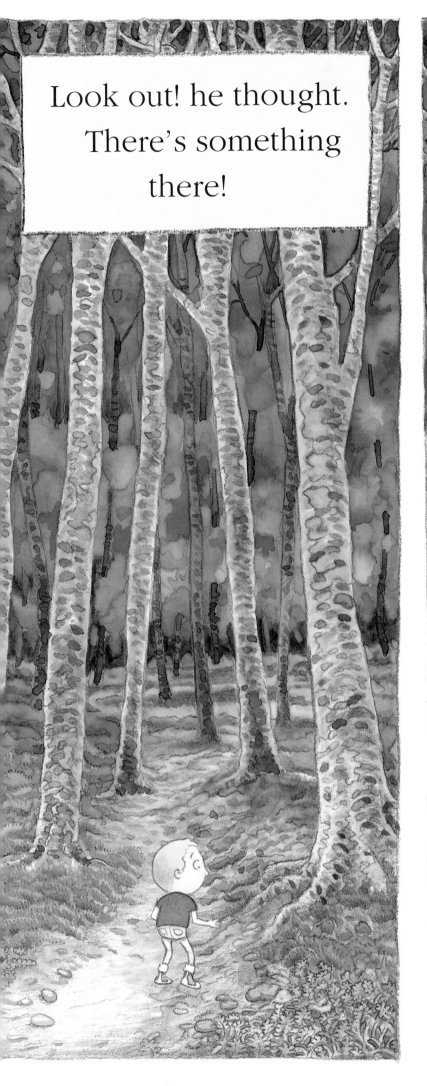

Look out! he thought.
There's something
there!

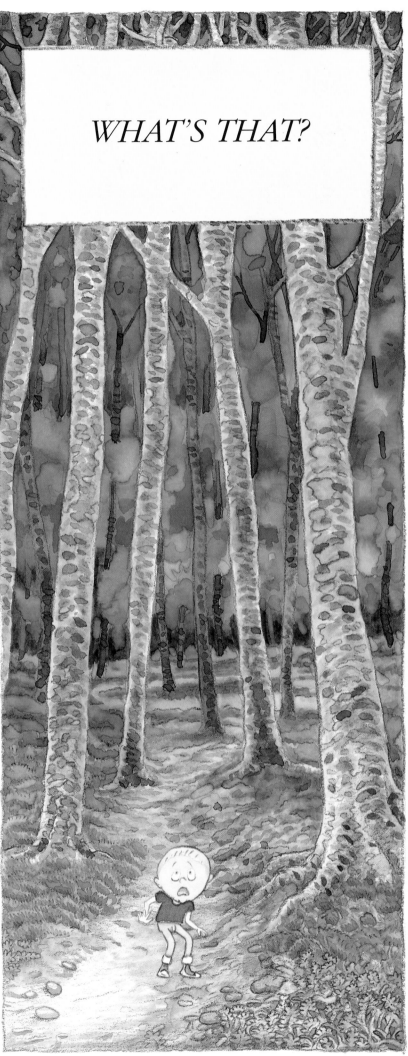

WHAT'S THAT?

A GIANT TEDDY BEAR!
"Is it Freddy?" said Eddy.
"What a surprise!
How *did* you get to be this size?"

"You're too big to huddle and cuddle," he said,

"and I'll never fit both of us into my bed."

Then out of the darkness,
clearer and clearer,
the sound of a sobbing
came nearer and nearer.

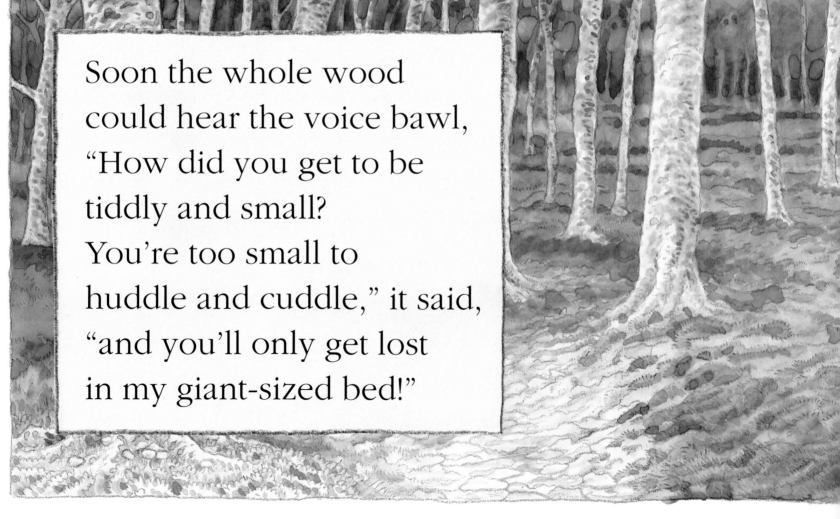

Soon the whole wood
could hear the voice bawl,
"How did you get to be
tiddly and small?
You're too small to
huddle and cuddle," it said,
"and you'll only get lost
in my giant-sized bed!"

It was a gigantic bear
and a tiddly teddy
stomping towards …

the giant teddy and Eddy.

"MY TED!"
gasped the bear.
"A BEAR!"
screamed Eddy.

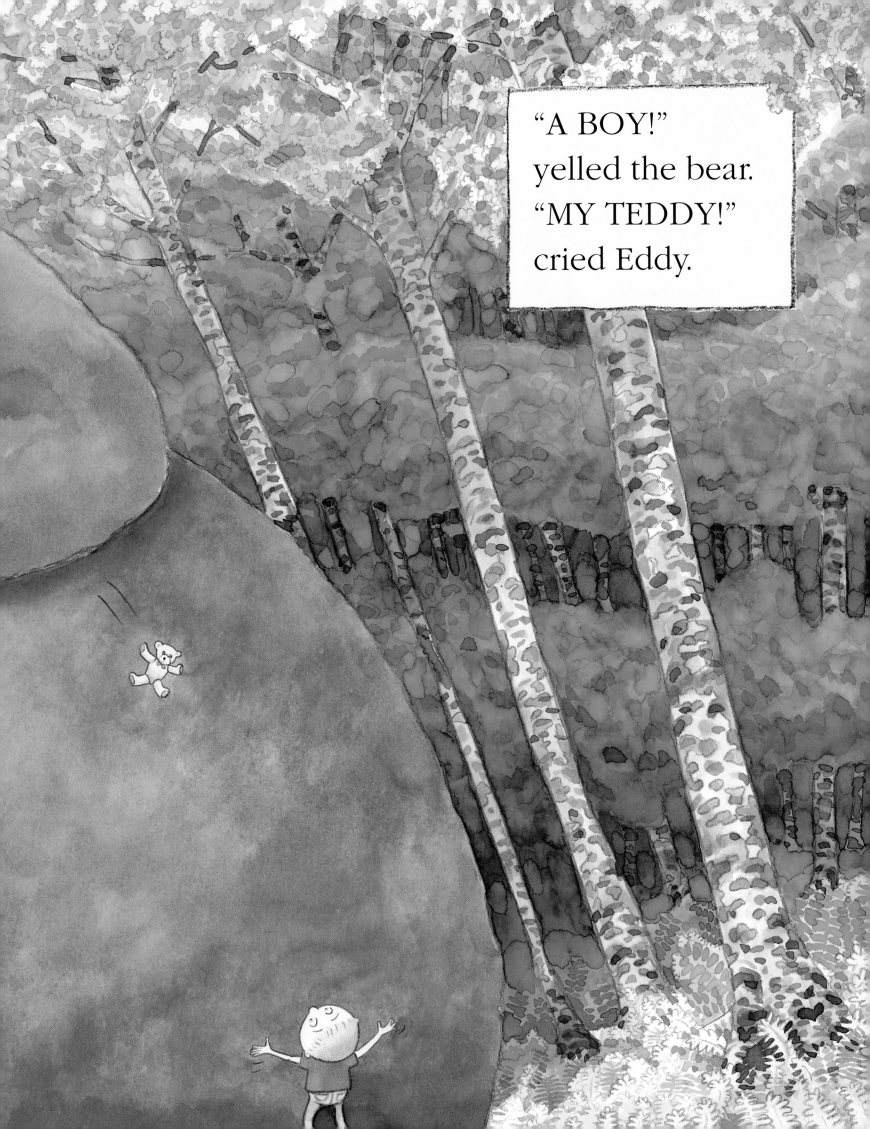

"A BOY!"
yelled the bear.
"MY TEDDY!"
cried Eddy.

Then they ran and they ran
through the dark wood
back to their homes
as quick as they could ...

all the way back
to their snuggly beds,
where they huddled
and cuddled their
own little teds.

For David, Amelia,
Jane, Jason and Lucy
with thanks

IT'S THE BEAR!

Eddy doesn't want to come
and picnic in the woods with Mum.

"I'm scared," he said, "about the bear,
the great big bear that lives in there."

"A bear?" said Mum. "That's silly, dear!
We don't get great big bears round here."

"There's just you and me and your teddy, Freddy.
Now let's all get the picnic ready."

"We've got lettuce,
tomatoes,
creamy cheese spread,
with hard-boiled eggs
and crusty brown bread.
There's orange juice,
biscuits,
some crisps and –

OH MY!

I've forgotten to pack
the blueberry pie..."

"I'll pop back and get it,"
she said. "Won't be long."
"BUT MUM!"
gasped Eddy …

too late –
SHE HAD GONE!

He sat on the hamper and tried not to cry, then…

"I CAN SMELL FOOD!" yelled a voice from nearby.

"*IT'S THE BEAR!*"
cried Eddy.
"*WHERE CAN I HIDE?*"

Then he opened
the hamper and
clambered inside.

Out of the trees
stepped a big hungry bear,
licking his lips
and sniffing the air.
"A teddy bear's picnic,"
he bellowed. "Hooray!"
"Help," whispered Eddy.
"He's coming this way."

He cuddled
his teddy,
he huddled
and hid ...

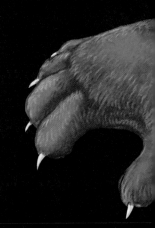

then a great big
bear bottom

sat down on the lid.

The bear munched
and he crunched,
he chomped
and he chewed,
and greedily gobbled up
all of the food.

"Now what's for dessert?"
said the bear.
    "Let me see..."

"Oh, please,"
whimpered Eddy,
"don't let it be me."

"Don't let him see me!
DON'T LET HIM COME..."

"HELP!"

shouted Eddy.

"Eddy, I'm coming," called Mum. "Are you hurt?"
"It's the bear," cried Eddy. "He thinks I'm dessert!"

"A bear?" said Mum. "I told you, my dear.
Your Freddy's the only bear round here."

"NO HE'S NOT!"
screamed Eddy.
*"BEHIND YOU,
IT'S THERE!"*
"Don't be silly,"
said Mum.
"There can't
be …
there just
can't be …
there isn't …"

"I *TOLD* you!" cried Eddy.
"RUN!" shouted Mum.
"Blueberry pie," said the bear.
"I *LOVE* it…"